CRAYON

For Erin and Isla

SIMON AND SCHUSTER
First published in Great Britain in 2014 by Simon and Schuster UK Ltd
1st Floor, 222 Gray's Inn Road, London WC1X 8HB
A CBS Company
Text and illustrations copyright © 2014 Simon Rickerty
The right of Simon Rickerty to be identified as the author and illustrator of this work has been
asserted by him in accordance with the Copyright, Designs and Patents Act, 1988
All rights reserved, including the right of reproduction in whole or in part in any form
A CIP catalogue record for this book is available from the British Library upon request
ISBN: 978-1-4711-1678-0 (HB)
ISBN: 978-1-4711-1679-7 (PB)
ISBN: 978-1-4711-1680-3 (eBook)
Printed in China
10 9 8 7 6 5 4 3 2 1

CRAYON

by Simon Rickerty

SIMON AND SCHUSTER
London   New York   Sydney   Toronto   New Delhi

Look!
Blue!

Look!
Red!

Hee hee.
Look what I'm doing!

Blue?
On my side?!

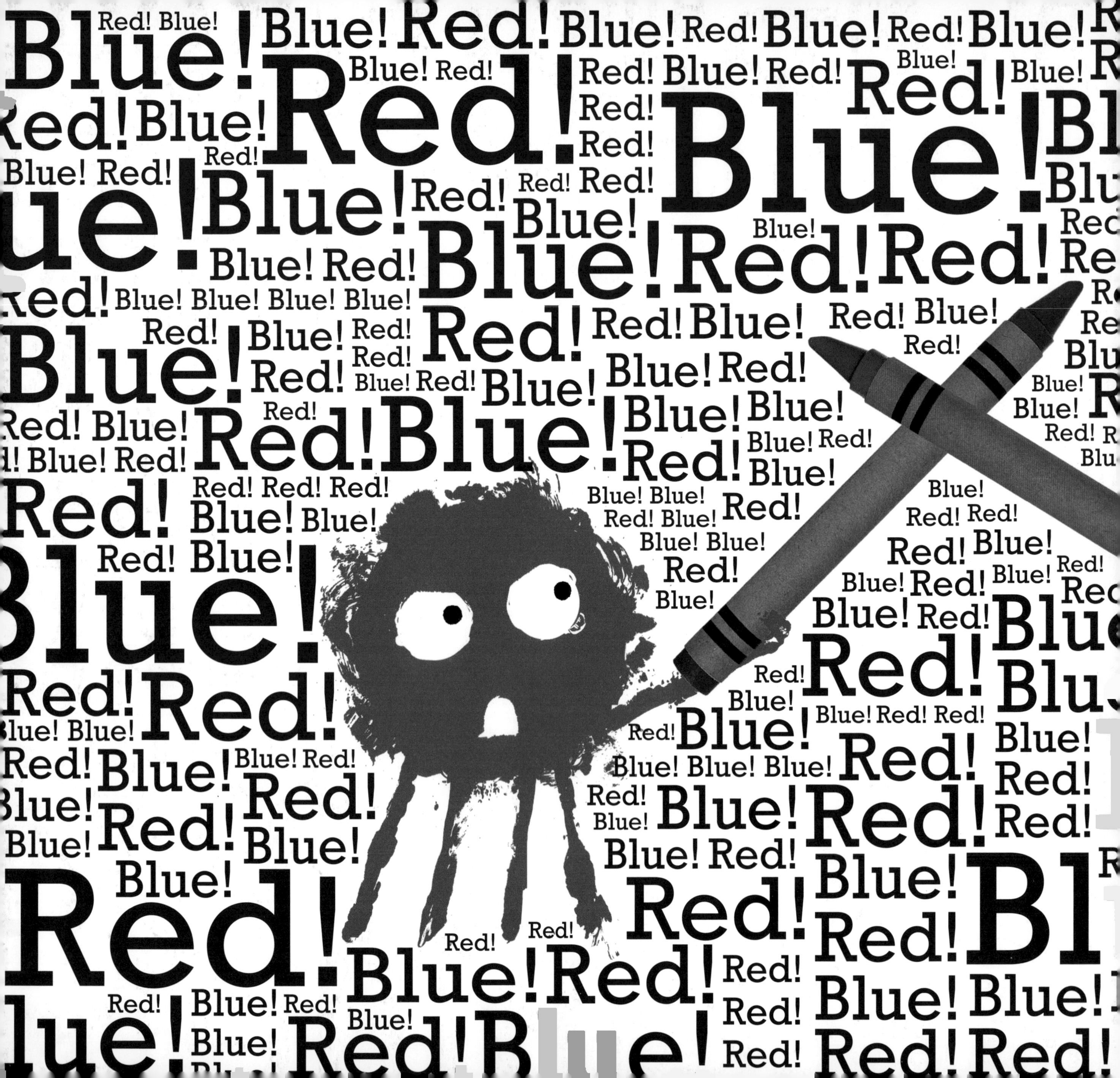

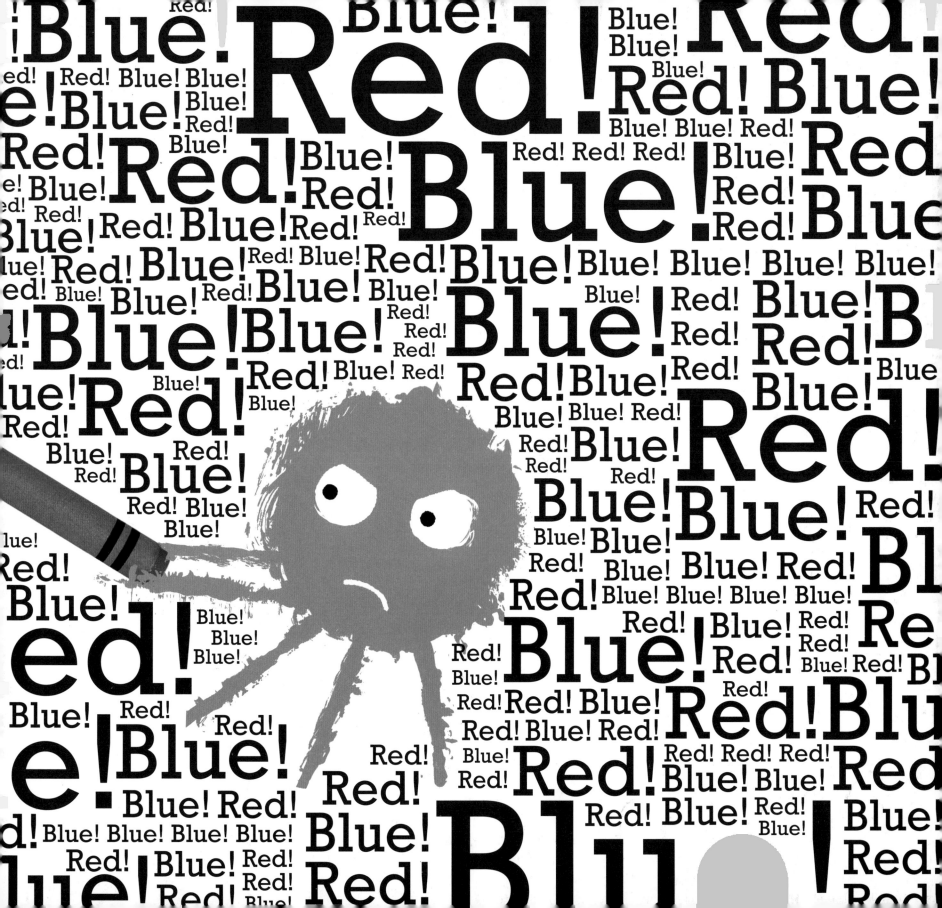

Stop!

Oh.
Oops.

Take my red.

Hee hee!
Now you're . . .

Purple!

Did
you
say
Purple?

Wow!

Purple . . .

Sniff, sniff.

Now for some orange.

A bit of brown.

And green . . .

And now we need . . .

Red!